GLADIATOR

The Story of a Fighter

Dee Phillips

READZONE

READZONE

First published in this edition 2013

ReadZone Books Limited
50 Godfrey Avenue
Twickenham
TW2 7PF
UK

The right of the Author to be identified as the Author of this work has been asserted by the Author in accordance with the Copyright, Designs and Patents Act 1988

Every attempt has been made by the Publisher to secure appropriate permissions for material reproduced in this book. If there has been any oversight we will be happy to rectify the situation in future editions or reprints. Written submissions should be made to the Publishers.

British Library Cataloguing in Publication Data (CIP) is available for this title.

ISBN 978-1-78322-009-0

Printed in China

Developed and Created by Ruby Tuesday Books Ltd
Project Director – Ruth Owen
Designer – Elaine Wilkinson

Images courtesy of Alamy (pages 25, 37), Rex Features (page 43), Shutterstock and Superstock (page 25).

Acknowledgements
With thanks to Lorraine Petersen, Chief Executive of NASEN, for her help in the development and creation of these books

Visit our website: www.readzonebooks.com

We waited deep below the arena.

I could smell blood.

Then it was my turn.

Marcus said, "Kill or be killed, Little Warrior."

GLADIATOR

The Story of a Fighter

In AD43, the Romans invaded Britain.

Many of the Celtic tribes in Britain fought against the invasion.

The Roman army was too powerful, however.

Many Celtic warriors were killed.

Others were taken prisoner.
Some warriors were sent to
Rome to become…

…GLADIATORS

My sword slashes through
skin and bone.
I hear the crowd cheering.
I can smell blood.
Kill or be killed.

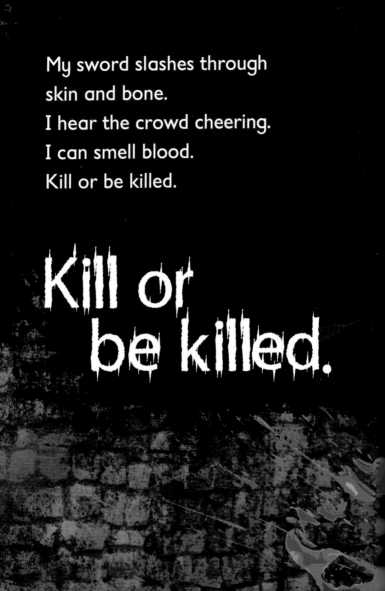

Kill or
be killed.

I wake up.

I am shaking.

There is no cheering crowd.

There is no blood.

I see mountains, trees and grass.

I am nearly home.

Today I will see my tribe again.

I think of my friend, Marcus.

I say, "Thank you, my friend."

My father was the king of our tribe.
He was a warrior.
I think of my father after a battle.
He has blood on his hands.

The heads of our enemies are on spikes.
Their village is burning.

When I was 15 I went to battle.
I fought next to my father.
I was small and fast.
I killed three men.

Our tribe won the battle.
My father was pleased.
He said, "You will be a good king
when I am dead."

Then the Romans came.

I start walking.
The mountains loom over me.
I am nearly home.
It has been five years.
But today I will see my tribe again.

Today, their king returns.

The Romans came to take our land.
Our tribe attacked the Romans.
I fought next to my father.

I was small and fast.
I killed many Romans but
it was not enough.
There were too many of them.

The battle lasted for many hours.
Then it happened.
A Roman spear flew through the air.
It landed in my father's back.
My father lay dying in the mud.
I tried to run to him.
But I was knocked to the ground.

I heard a voice. "Tie him up!"
An old soldier on a horse looked
down at me.
The old soldier said, "You fight
well, little Briton."
He said, "You will fight for me
back in Rome."

I shouted, "I will never fight for a Roman!"
The old soldier laughed.

"Kill or be killed, Little Warrior."

I walk all day.
The mountains loom over me.
I was in Rome for five years.
But I am nearly home.

I think of my friend, Marcus.
I say, "Thank you, my friend."

I was the Romans' prisoner.
I was sent to a school for gladiators.
By day we trained to fight using
different types of weapons.
At night we were locked in prison cells.

Marcus was the Romans' prisoner, too.
He came from a land far from Rome.
Marcus was a champion gladiator.
Every day we trained.
I said, "I have to go home. My tribe needs their king."

Marcus laughed, "You are a gladiator,
Little Warrior, not a king.
You will die here in Rome."

Soon, my gladiator training
was over.
We waited deep below the arena.
I could smell blood.
A prisoner screamed as lions
ripped him apart.
The crowd cheered.
Then it was my turn.
Marcus said, "Kill or be killed,
Little Warrior."

I walked into the arena.
A huge gladiator was waiting.
The crowd laughed.
"Fight, Little Warrior," they shouted.

The laughing soon stopped.

I was small and fast.
My sword slashed through skin and bone.
The huge gladiator lay dying in the sand.
Kill or be killed.
I was a gladiator now.

The sun is going down.
I am nearly home.
I have come back to my tribe.
I have come to be their king.

"Thank you, Marcus. Thank you, my friend, for saving my life."

Marcus and I were the best gladiators in Rome.
Soon I was the old soldier's champion.
Marcus said, "I knew you would be a champion
Little Warrior."
But I wanted to go home.

I hated Rome.
I hated the Romans.
I trusted no one but Marcus.

The years passed.

Cheering crowds...
the smell of blood...
my sword slashing
through skin and bone.

I said to the old soldier, "I want
to go home. I want my freedom."

The old soldier smiled.
"One last fight. Then you will
have your freedom."

The day of my last fight came.
I walked into the arena.
A gladiator was waiting.
The old soldier looked down on us.
He laughed, "Fight for your freedom,
little Briton."

I turned to my friend.
"I will not fight you," I said.

Marcus lifted his sword.

He said, "It is time for you to go home.
Kill or be killed, my friend."

The mountains loom over me.
I can see my tribe's village.
An old woman sees me.
She screams my name.
People run from their huts.
They shout and cheer for their king.
I am home.
I think of my friend, Marcus.
I say, "Thank you, brave gladiator."

GLADIATORS:

Behind the Story

In Roman times, over 2,000 years ago, people liked watching gladiators kill each other. Spectators sat in huge, open-air arenas, like sports stadiums today.

Gladiators were usually criminals, slaves, or prisoners of war. These men, and sometimes women, were trained at gladiator schools to fight each other to the death.

During training, gladiators used blunt weapons and wooden swords. In real contests, they used sharp metal daggers, swords and weapons like huge forks, called tridents.

Gladiators usually lived together at the school. They were fed bread and porridge made from boiled barley. At night, they were locked in their cells. There was no escape!

A Day at the Arena
- In the morning, hunters fought and killed wild animals such as lions, crocodiles and bears.
- At midday, executions took place. Criminals were tied to posts and then torn apart by wild animals.
- In the afternoon, pairs of gladiators fought until one was killed.

Once a gladiator was trained, a rich Roman could hire the fighter from the school. The gladiator then fought as that person's champion in gladiator contests.

A scene from the movie, *Gladiator*.

43

THANK YOU, MY FRIEND
ON YOUR OWN

Thank you, my friend

Imagine you are Little Warrior back home after five years in Rome. Write a letter or a poem to your friend, Marcus.
Think about:

• How is Little Warrior feeling – sad, guilty, happy to be home?

KILL OR BE KILLED
ON YOUR OWN / WITH A PARTNER / IN A GROUP

Think about or discuss the book:

• How do you think it felt to be made to fight as a gladiator?

• How did Little Warrior and Marcus feel before each fight?

• Did you guess that one day the two friends would have to fight each other?

Do you think Marcus allowed his friend, Little Warrior, to win their last fight, or did Marcus truly fight to the death? Discuss what you think happened.

- Did Marcus sacrifice himself for his friend's future?

- Did Little Warrior win because he was driven by his desire to go home?

OUTSIDERS
WITH A PARTNER

When the Roman army invaded an area, they built forts and sometimes towns. In time, the soldiers and local people learned to live together. Imagine that when Little Warrior returns to his village, he discovers his sister is now married to a Roman! With a partner, role-play the conversation they have.

- How does Little Warrior feel about Romans living alongside his people?

- Does he ask his sister to choose between him and her husband?

- Think of a way that the brother and sister's story might take place in the modern world.

Titles in the
Yesterday's Voices
series

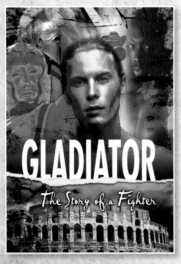

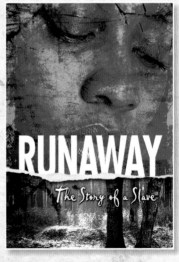

I waited deep below the arena.
Then it was my turn to fight.
Kill or be killed!

I cannot live as a slave
any longer. Tonight, I will
escape and never go back.

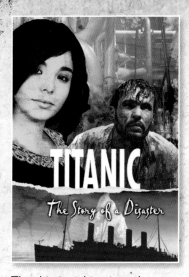

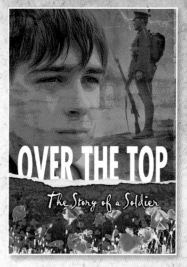

The ship is sinking into the icy sea. I don't want to die. Someone help us!

I'm waiting in the trench. I am so afraid. Tomorrow we go over the top.

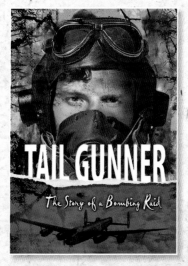

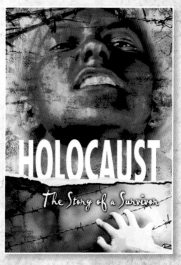

Another night. Another bombing raid. Will this night be the one when we don't make it back?

They took my clothes and shaved my head. I was no longer a human.